I0788550

PRAISE FOR JUSTINE AVERY

"A sweetly-written page-turner.... highly recommended."

— *The Wishing Shelf Book Awards*

"A tantalizingly human story. You'll recognize all the clumsy, embarrassing things we think, say and do and then desperately try to cover up ... while in pursuit of love.... we discover that love was something we thought we lacked and desperately wanted but it was already ours all along."

— Loretta M. Siani, author of *Everyday Miracles: Nine Keys to Miraculous Living*

"A really sweet short story. A lot of punch behind a powerful moral in such a short number of pages.... I know which outcome I was rooting for and my wish came true."

— Brit Rossie, *Readers' Favorite*

THE POST-IT NOTE AFFAIR

A ROMANCE NOVELETTE OF LOVE LOST AND FOUND

JUSTINE AVERY

ISBN: 978-1-948124-99-7
ISBN: 978-1-948124-98-0 (paperback)
ASIN: B015LLTSIM (ebook)
ISBN: 9781948124157 (audio book)

Chapter 1

hat exactly is love? Is it the words said aloud? Thoughts shared or even just the ones you keep to yourself? Is it the activities you do with someone, the time you spend together? Is it the things you live through: the hardships, happinesses, the ups and downs? Or is it all just your imagination?

You can't see love. You can't touch it. And sometimes, it just completely floats away, out of your grasp; and then, it's gone, almost as quickly and surprisingly as it first came.

If love really is just all in our minds, why do we miss it so much when it's gone? Why does it feel like a favorite warm and fuzzy blanket we love to stay wrapped up in as long as possible; and then, we feel so insecure and vulnerable—utterly alone—when we're no longer bundled in it?

I miss my blanket. Maybe that's why a little square of happy-yellow paper just *affected* me so much. Kind of embarrassing actually—if it wasn't for how deliciously wonderful it was to just discover that little surprise and feel *excited* again. Even if just for a moment.

I'll take those moments. Please, please give me more.

I don't know what I thought marriage was going to be. Wait, of course, I do. And I admit it. I totally fell for the "happily ever after," just as I fell for Stephen. It was so easy—dreamy, even.

We were high school sweethearts, then college sweethearts, then we married. It made complete sense, and I couldn't imagine life any other way or with anyone else. We're just so *compatible*—I know, not very exciting but nicely comfortable.

We just *work*. Maybe because we're from the same town, our family members and friends all know each other, we grew together, or we've just come to really know and understand each other over the years.

But maybe that's why it's just gotten, well, *boring*. Living with Stephen is like having a really great pet. Did I just *think* that? He's everything you could want in a companion. He has those big puppy-dog eyes, he's cute, friendly, fun, full of energy, a great listener, and he utterly adores me. But there are some things he just can't offer.

You know what I'm talking about. Where's the oomph, the thrill, the fireworks, the romance? Did we ever have it, or were we just in a youthful daze or too shy or scared or whatever to seek it?

One thing's for sure: my husband just doesn't *do it* for me. Not anymore. I love him, but that old flame and spark have long since been extinguished. And I've stopped trying to rekindle it. How many times can a woman try to spell it all out, making herself vulnerable, and practically write down *instructions* for how she wants to be treated, wooed, loved, before she starts to feel pathetic for even needing to?

And Stephen does try. I have to give him credit for that.

He does care; that's obvious. And just admitting that I want *more* makes me feel completely guilty. I'm not ungrateful. I'm just not ready to give up on feeling really, truly *desired.* I'm not ready to give up my right to tingles, thrills, and butterflies. And for all of my husband's great qualities, dependability, and real love for me, Stephen just can't provide that package.

I want the total package: the pretty box with the big red bow *and* the sparkly, shiny thing inside.

So, what does that have to do with a silly little piece of pale yellow paper? Well, I'll tell you. That otherwise inconspicuous and completely unimportant sticky-edged Post-it I found wading in the depths of my purse one rushed morning *made my day.*

And I had no idea the profound effect it was going to have on my whole life.

Chapter 2

It was a Monday, another horrible Monday. I was late to get to work after being late to leave the house and late to reach the I-465. I was late to pick up my morning coffee, late to my desk, and too late to make it look like I'd actually arrived at the office on time.

I scrounged around in my bag for who-knows-what when my fingertips touched what I thought was a bit of trash, a piece of wrinkled paper that didn't belong in my purse at all. That made me angry—like *everything* did on days that started the way that Monday did.

I pulled it out, crushed it into a ball, and was about to toss it at the wastebasket at the far end of my desk when I paused for a moment and my brain finally kicked in. *Why would there be something in my bag that I didn't put there?*

In those two seconds, I was actually logical. And my life changed like the flick of a switch.

I uncrumpled the paper and realized something was scribbled on it: a handwritten note, just a couple words, in bold block letters.

YOU'RE TERRIFIC!

That was it. Nothing more. But it was enough.

Was it the word "terrific" or the "you" that made me feel like the note could actually be intended for me, meant as a compliment? Or was it the in-your-face effect of the exclamation mark itself? Someone chose to use that exclamation mark. Someone seriously meant what he or she wrote.

But it couldn't be for me. My name wasn't on it. It wasn't signed or anything. It could even be a joke. Or a stray scrap piece of paper accidentally swallowed up by my purse: shrapnel from a paper wad fight over the cubicle walls. And that could've been days or even weeks ago.

I looked over the front wall of my cubicle then, trying to remember an incident that could've produced a stray bit of paper in my purse. Then, I realized how much time I was wasting letting my mind wander as if the Post-it was the center of the world's greatest unsolved mystery. So, I reprimanded myself to add to my Monday morning stress, and dropped the paper note in the wastebasket.

Five minutes later, I pulled it out again. And pinned it to the cubicle wall, right above my computer monitor.

There it was, all day long. That big, bold "TERRIFIC" stared directly at me, demanding my attention no matter what went on around me. If one of my coworkers mumbled anything I thought was directed at me, that "TERRIFIC" just erased it from my mind just as fast. If I wondered if I had any real friends in the office at all, that "you" singled me out and made me feel like someone was paying attention to me and recognized that I existed, that I was someone worth writing to. And that poignant exclamation mark—as silly as it seems—forced a smile on my face so many times during the day. The note was like a little secret friend whisper-shouting at me and cheekily prodding me to cheer up—demanding it.

And I didn't even know if that Post-it note really was meant for me.

That afternoon, I practically glided out of the office as if I didn't have a care in the world. Instead of focusing on all the annoying faces, pointless meetings, and tiring tasks, the one thing at the forefront of my mind was that little note, that happy little yellow note.

The long commute home seemed to fly by, and when I walked through the door, I spontaneously smiled at Stephen. No particular reason, except that I just felt different, happier. And he smiled back. No hesitation, just that boyish grin that used to make me gush when I was a teenager and even into our honeymoon years. And it didn't even annoy me.

I brought piles of work home with me, but that didn't bother me either. I just felt—through and through and undeniably—well, *terrific*. Just because a casual little note instructed me to.

And it probably wasn't even meant for me. How could it be? Who in the world would bother? Passing notes is a school day pastime—for kids. Girlfriends are great for a perky pick-me-up, but they'd just say it out loud. Coworkers just aren't that considerate. And, as for the office climate, management certainly hasn't adopted a scheme for boosting morale in the workplace that involves scribbling down peppy mottos of positivity.

Whoever it was meant for, it was mine now: my own personal reminder that there are surprises in the world, and you never know when or where you might find them. That was enough for me; that was more fun than I had in a long time.

Chapter 3

The next morning, I still felt different, though I didn't remember why. I wasn't too grumpy when the alarm yanked me out of a great dream, and I paused to lean over and leave a quick kiss on sleeping Stephen's cheek before I pulled myself out of bed. He looks so young and sweet when he sleeps: the very same face of the boy I fell for. No matter what happened, what dragged us down or confronted us in our shared life or what kind of day I had or mood I woke up in, Stephen was always right there, sleeping soundly, reminding me that everything must be okay. If nothing else—if our marriage wasn't meant for anything more—at least I had one friend in the world, one person that was always on my side.

Some days, that was enough. Most days, I couldn't help but hunger for more. Should I really be ashamed of that?

That morning, I felt like putting in a little extra effort. I took the time for a few extra touches of makeup. I bothered to pick out a workday ensemble that made me feel just a bit more together, a bit more fashionable, a bit more feminine. After all, I actually woke up with the first round of the alarm. I might've momentarily forgotten there was a snooze button.

I strolled into work proud of the fact that I arrived on time. Of course, no one seemed to notice. I didn't even get a prize for that. There should be prizes for that.

I plopped my purse on my desk, fished out a few start-of-the-day necessities, and slid into my swiveling chair. I noticed the Post-it right away—exactly where I'd pinned it the day before—and it made me smile again.

I actually felt terrific. I could get used to it.

I decided I should start the workday with a break. I could brew up a fresh pot of coffee in the break room, browse the take-out menus and look forward to lunch. Why not?

I was staring at the brown mass clinging to the filter in the top of the coffee machine when a man's voice startled me, almost causing me to bang my head on the upper cabinet. "Need some help with that?"

I spun around, ready to say something snippy to cover up my embarrassment, when a pair of sharp blue eyes stole my attention. My mouth might've even hung open, ready to speak if it wasn't for the fact that all other thoughts were instantly erased from my mind.

He just stood there, those intense eyes looking into mine, a partial smile on his face. I'd never seen him before in my life. And I really regretted it.

"I just wondered... if you wanted some help... with the coffee machine?" His dirty blonde hair was long enough to just touch his ears and the collar of his shirt at the back of his neck. That shirt fit him very well, and the gray pinstripes looked amazing as a backdrop for his ocean-blue eyes. "I'm... Josh," he said, reaching out his hand.

My manners kicked in to save me, triggering my reflexes

to raise my own hand to shake his. His handshake was warm, firm, but not too strong and showy. I instantly liked him.

My smile happened without a thought; I hoped it wasn't too warm or weird. "Nice to meet you, Josh. I'm Emily. And... I'm okay with the coffee machine, thanks. It's just... gross."

He chuckled a little bit: a warm, easy kind of chuckle. I wanted to chuckle like that.

Blue-eyed Josh stepped closer to me, and my body temperature literally rose a few degrees. I couldn't confirm that I remembered to roll on the antiperspirant that morning—suddenly my biggest worry in the world.

"Let me take it on," Josh said, his eyes focused on the coffee machine behind me. Take on—take *off*—my mind wandered uncontrollably. "I need to earn my keep around here," he said, only adding to my intense, impromptu discomfort.

When he spoke again, I realized I hadn't moved out of his way. "I'm sorry. Am I being too forward?"

I stood there like a crazy woman; I gripped the break room counter like it was the only thing separating me from a fatal drop off the roof of a high-rise building. And my face hurt. For some godforsaken reason, I'd scrunched up so tight that I must've looked like I was suffering acute pain.

"No. I..." I released my hold on the counter and stepped out of the man's way. "Sorry. Distracted. Too much work. You know." I squeezed a smile onto my tense face.

"Do they work you that hard here? Thanks for the warning." He flashed his easy smile again, pouring with more confidence than I ever had. Half of me secretly wished he'd stop smiling, stop making my skin feel so hot. The other half dared, *do it again.*

I watched his hands finesse the coffee machine, expertly

clean out the reservoir, and attend to detail like I've never seen a man do. I noticed the perfect fit of his slacks as his back was turned to me. I reached for a coffee mug to pretend like I was doing something else—anything but noticing how attractive he was. The rings on my wedding finger that I usually barely noticed, that had become such a part of my own body—my own identity—suddenly felt so *heavy.*

"So... you're new here?" I asked in a desperate attempt to hide everything I felt at the moment.

Josh turned to face me. I noticed his dress shirt pulled tight across his muscular shoulder as he twisted at the waist. "You noticed," he said with his eyes sparkling.

Why did everything coming out of his mouth sound like flirting to me? I couldn't even enjoy the moment, could barely allow myself to feel like an attractive woman again, because every second in that break room only pointed out how severely deprived I was, how lackluster my marriage was. Why didn't my husband's words and compliments make my skin sizzle like that?

"Yeah, I'm the new guy. Marketing," Josh said. "And you?"

"Sales," I proudly managed to answer with socially expected timing.

"Oh, then we'll probably be seeing more of each other."

My skin burst into flames. I lifted the coffee mug to my lips, tipped it, then pretended to take a sip—and swallow— as I remembered there was nothing in it.

"Well, it's good to go now. Should be a much better brew this time. Possibly the best this office has ever had."

"Probably," I tried to say casually.

"Want the first taste?"

I slowly nodded, holding on to the empty mug like my life depended on it, missing the security of the counter.

"May I have it?" he asked.

My admiration? My undying devotion? My virtue? My fidelity?

"The coffee mug," he said.

Waking out of my daydream, I practically shoved the mug at him. Josh's lips parted to say something, then he just smiled and turned around again to pour the first cup.

I took the opportunity to start breathing again, practically panting at him while his back was turned, and I quickly closed my mouth again as he delivered the fresh coffee. It smelled amazing.

"How do you take it?" His voice was so firm and dominant.

I prayed he couldn't read the thought that flashed across my mind.

"Milk? Sugar?" he asked.

I shook my head.

"Straight up?" He actually looked impressed. "Nice. Me too."

I think I smiled. My face felt tight. I just couldn't tell. I couldn't think.

Was it just me, or did we both feel the electric tension in the air? I could almost hear it, like the drone of static beating at my eardrums.

"Well, I better get back to my desk. It was a pleasure making coffee for you," Josh said, and he seemed to mean it.

"Thank you," I managed to speak in a normal manner. "Hope you... like it here," I added just to ensure he left with the impression that I was inexplicably strange.

Then, he chuckled again, and I felt every muscle in my body relax. Just a little bit. I wanted to live in Josh's world, where he probably woke up looking perfect, faced every day with complete confidence, seemed to view the workday as stress-free and full of wonder, and he laughed and smiled so easily.

"I already do," he answered, and he stepped past me, staring directly into my eyes. And with the slightest, most casual and questionably accidental brush of his sleeve against mine. I felt the fabric of my blouse brush my arm as if it was Josh's own skin. I was incredibly grateful that he was finally leaving so I could melt in peace.

"Oh, Emily..." he mentioned just as he stepped outside the break room.

"Yes?" I said, way too eagerly, as I spun around on my high heels.

"By the way, you look... *terrific*," he said with a certain kind of smile I'll never forget. And he vanished down the corridor.

I stumbled, the surface of my coffee swaying danger-ously near the edge of the mug, and can't say that I was anything like my normal self the rest of the day.

I tried to stay in my cubicle all day, to hide from any possible chance encounters I just didn't have the sanity to deal with, but I also buzzed with new energy. I couldn't sit still; I felt alive. For the first time in too long.

I went through spurts of furious work and serious effi-ciency between bouts of giddy, girlish excitement and peeks, of course, at my beloved Post-it hanging in front of me. I relished the coincidence of Josh's choice of word in his compliment while I fully acknowledged it *was* just a coinci-dence. After all, if it wasn't, there was no doubt at all in my mind then that I would *not* be able to handle it. Not that same day. Probably not ever.

Then came the chance to prove it to myself.

I was staring at the sales strategy document for the new fiscal quarter on my computer monitor when a much too familiar voice spoke over my cubicle wall. That voice was almost more recognizable than my own husband's—because I'd been replaying it in my mind about every ten minutes since my morning coffee.

"So, this is where you hide," he said. And suddenly, the little recurring scene in my head, which almost seemed like just a fantasy, continued on.

I turned in my chair just enough to face him. Josh's eyes were even more striking than my memory of them.

"Hello," I said, miraculously managing a calm, friendly smile.

"Hi again. How was your coffee?"

"Oh, just fine, thank you. Definitely the best this office has ever had."

"Great! Maybe they'll keep me around for a while then."

"I hope so," I said way too quickly and just before mentally slapping myself.

His stare honed in on me, started to warm my skin again. And that incredible smile slowly pointed at his dimples again.

He didn't make a joke of my forward reply, although it begged for it. He didn't belittle my confession at all; instead, he preserved it. He made it our little secret, sealing it with "me too."

I blushed then. I felt it rush to my cheeks. My outfit—my *new favorite* outfit—felt excruciatingly tight. I wiggled in my seat, crossed my legs more rigidly, looked down at the dirty-gray carpeting like a shy schoolgirl.

"Well, I'm glad I found you," he said in a volume sounding less suspicious to any eavesdroppers. "You're the only one that's said a word to me. Besides the boss. And the ladies in HR. And the guy in the office next to mine. Oh, and the cleaning lady. She accidentally walked in on me when I was in the restroom. I guess I... I'm too quiet."

I laughed. Way too loudly. I used it to disguise my need to finally breathe.

"I better get back to it," he said, and I felt a bit sad. "But be warned. I know where you are now." He smiled, slid his hands off the top of my cubicle wall, and walked silently away.

A full five minutes passed before I realized I was staring at the top of my desk. I hadn't moved since Josh left. My throat was dry. I didn't even remember what I'd been daydreaming about. But I could guess.

I rolled my chair over slightly and reached for my purse sitting on the desktop. I scrounged around for a bottle of water and drank nearly half of it. When I gently laid it back on top of the contents of my purse, my fingernail caught the edge of a piece of paper.

I glanced around; no one looked in my direction. I felt like I'd been given a very special gift, intended just for me, and I hadn't even seen it yet.

The surprise in my purse, mysteriously placed there by someone else's hand, was pale blue this time and neatly folded: a Post-it sealed on its sticky side, hinting of the need for secrecy. My pulse raced, the anticipation made everything else around me fade out of existence, and I remembered how exciting it was to pass notes in class behind the teacher's back when I was a little girl—especially the return of one reading "Do you like me? Check 'Yes' or 'No.'"

That's exactly how I felt. I could've never opened the inconspicuous note—I could've been happy just savoring the anticipation itself—but I couldn't pass up the chance at more.

I found just four little words, quickly jotted down in block letters:

I LOVE
YOUR SMILE

Black ink on soft blue paper, pretty and full of affection. At least, that's what I convinced myself.

There was no doubt in my mind, this time, that the note was meant for me. My purse couldn't be an accidental receptacle for someone else's discarded messages *twice*. And you know who was just at my desk, his gorgeous face hovering over my handbag. And *he* thought I looked terrific. He said it. He said *that* word.

But it wasn't Josh I focused on as I studied the new note in my hands. I was moved by the very choice of words.

This note was so much more personal, beginning with "I." The mention of my smile, well, that was very intimate, flattering, shiver-inducing. And the word "love" scribbled by someone's hand—that was a game-changer. That was the big leagues.

This was full-on flirting: a very intimate compliment delivered in a very private way. I had no idea what to do—*if* I should do anything or say anything. Was I supposed to write back?

No, I didn't want to ruin it. I didn't want to make it complicated. Life was complicated enough. What I wanted —what I really longed for—was the sweet and simple. I just wanted to feel *good*. I just wanted that thrill of discovery, possibility, of someone's *attention* to last forever. Just the way it was.

At home that night, I practically ran into Stephen's arms. I just felt so *guilty*. I buried my face in the crook of his neck, wanting to reassure him—and myself?—that I hadn't done anything wrong and also needing to feel that stability. I was practically spinning all day at work since the break room encounter; I needed to know that the rest of my life—my real life—was still waiting there for me, that I hadn't taken a misstep or crossed a line. I hugged my husband for permission to feel good about myself, to allow myself to enjoy the attention that made me feel like a woman again.

Even if it wasn't from Stephen.

Chapter 4

On the way into work the next day, I rode a rollercoaster of emotions on the commute, like experiencing a full, weepy dramatic film all in my head. I looked forward to the chance to receive a new secret note; I chastised myself for wanting one. I guessed at what my admirer might write next; I worried about what it would mean or what expectations might come with it. I drove myself absolutely nuts. Only one thing was really clear. Life was *interesting* again.

And once I survived a new day at the office without any little surprises spontaneously showing up in my purse or anywhere else, I cursed at myself for reading so much into them in the first place—for wanting them so badly, for letting them mean so much to me. They were just compliments, only simple little words—just notes, letters on a piece of cheap paper—and I was a silly little girl.

"How was your day?" Stephen asked innocently, genuinely, as he freed himself of his suit as I walked into the bedroom after another emotional day.

He had no idea what I'd been through, what was thrown

at me suddenly that week and all the questions I tortured myself with, but I knew he could read the worry behind my eyes. I knew he cared.

Stephen waited for me to answer. If I didn't, he'd ask again, assuming I didn't hear him the first time. He walked over to his side of the closet, carefully hung his suit pants on their hanger while standing there in just his shirt, underwear, and socks pulled up high on his calves. I must've been staring at them when he repeated his question.

"Emily... everything okay today at work?"

"Mmm, hmm," I mumbled with a nod, still focused on the spot on the carpet where he'd been standing.

Stephen sat on the bed next to me; I didn't even remember sitting down.

"What's the matter? Any horror stories you want to share? I'm all ears."

He couldn't know, but every time he said that phrase, I instantly thought of his ears. They were fine ears, but ears are funny things. Next thing I knew, I was thinking of ears, not of problems, and Stephen had done it again: worked his calming magic on me.

"Are you smiling?" he asked, flashing one of his own. "Well, that was easy. Want me to do dinner tonight?"

I looked up at my husband, sitting there in his underpants without a care in the world—except for my own happiness—and wondered what his secret was. What kept him so calm and happy all the time? Why was he so blissfully in love with someone who selfishly wanted more?

"Come on. I'll make you a hot cup of my special tea," he said, gently squeezing my hand and walking out of the bedroom without his pants.

I pushed myself back into my own comfortable life: free of surprises, good or bad.

Chapter 5

By the time a new week rolled around, I'd convinced myself I didn't really care about the two little notes. There wasn't a third. I never looked at the second one again; I was tired of thinking about it or wondering what it meant and hated myself for caring so much anyway.

The first Post-it still clung to my cubicle wall. I liked it. I liked the happy-yellow paper, kind of businessy but cheerful. I liked feeling terrific, even if I just pretended based on knowing someone else thought I was for a time.

And I hadn't seen the slightest glimpse of Josh for several days, not so much as a casual crossing of paths or any sign of a properly made carafe of coffee. Of course, I was mad at myself for caring; but those big blue eyes, that energizing smile, *did* something to me. Was it so wrong to like that feeling?

I decided I needed a change. Sometimes, that's all you ever need: a shopping spree or a new hobby. I opted for a new haircut.

On a whim, I treated myself to an extra long lunch hour

and squeezed in a visit to my hairstylist. I returned to the office with a new spring in my step and that great feeling of getting away with an unapproved, extended lunch.

I didn't do anything drastic to my usual low-maintenance look; that wasn't my style. Just a great trim and a little extra styling to pep me up. I didn't think anyone would notice; they weren't supposed to notice I took the time to do anything other than run through the drive-thru line.

Back at work, busily plugging formulas into an Excel spreadsheet, I thought I heard a knock behind me. When I spun around in my chair, Josh stood at the entrance to my cubicle.

His pale gray suit fit him perfectly, showing off the form of a man obviously focused on keeping in shape. The blue silk tie coordinated with his eyes rather than contrasted. *A woman* must *dress him.* The thought made me frown just as soon as it occurred to me.

"You've done something with your hair," he said, as if it was blatantly apparent.

"Uh, yeah... yes. How'd you..." I really wanted to know *where* he'd been. And if there'd be any more notes.

"It catches the light differently," he said, seeming to ponder the phenomenon even as he spoke. "Nice."

"Thanks."

"Would you believe..." he started, leaning on the cubicle wall. "That they sent me off to some off-site location for orientation? Something about the big meeting room here being refitted. I was trapped in a rented room with strangers for three whole days! I didn't think there'd be that much I needed to be *oriented* on, but apparently, there are *lots* of rules here."

"Yeah, I guess so. I wondered..." I stopped myself. Being the incidental recipient of gifted notes was one thing;

actively admitting I liked having him around was another—as a married woman.

"Wondered what?" he asked, cocking his head to the side.

"How you were doing. Being new and all."

"Great. Well, now that I'm back in the office around... the people I like."

We stared at each other a moment; we must have. And once again, he rescued me from complete embarrassment and awkwardness with an excuse to leave, perfectly preserving another shared moment.

And oh, how I reminisced over that moment the rest of the afternoon. I even caught another glimpse of Josh just before leaving for the day, just catching his gaze over the walls as he popped into a nearby cubicle—and his smile, the smile that made me sizzle inside.

Back at home again, I luxuriated in feeling like there was something—someone—fun at work to look forward to. I must've been grinning over dinner, because Stephen called me on it.

"What are you thinking about?"

"Nothing. Just work stuff."

"A funny story?"

"No."

"All right."

I could tell he was disappointed for not getting more out of me, but there was nothing worth telling him about, nothing that would interest him.

Before I crawled into bed with Stephen that night, I caught a peek of myself in the vanity mirror. I loved the subtle sassiness of my new trim, the way the shorter strands of hair accentuated my eyes. Then, I wondered why Stephen never said a word about it. He was never shy with compliments.

I slid under the bedcovers and sat up against the headboard, watching my husband finish the page he was reading.

"I can feel your eyes on me," he said. "Drilling holes in the back of my head."

"Am not."

"Yes, you are. I have a sixth sense. Especially when it comes to you."

No, I thought. *You don't know everything.*

Stephen closed his book and turned toward me. "What's up?"

"Nothing."

"Oh, so you want to play a game then? Let's see... you found my dirty socks outside of the laundry hamper instead of *inside*?"

"No!" I almost shouted, hoping my defensiveness wasn't that obvious.

"You want me to take your car tomorrow and fill it up for you?"

"That'd be nice... but no."

"I give up."

"You're usually much better at this game."

"So it *is* a game; you admit it!" Something about how proud he was of himself annoyed the heck out of me.

"That's not the point."

"Then, what is the point?" He wasn't angry; he never got angry. No matter how many times I'd tried—I'll admit—during our relationship, I could never drive him to anger, to make him as upset as I was in any given moment.

"The point *is*... I got my hair cut today, and *you* didn't notice!"

"Oh, that."

"Yes!" I didn't even know why I yelled the word.

"Looks great. Of course."

"You didn't even notice!"

"Of course, I did."

"Well, why didn't you say something?"

"I just did."

"Uh, Stephen!" I rolled over, turning my back on him.

"I love you, and I still will in the morning," he said, no malice at all in his voice. He switched off the bedside lamp, leaving me to fume alone in the dark.

Chapter 6

I really looked forward to reaching the office the next day, even if I wouldn't admit to myself all the reasons why. I walked in a bit taller, my re-energized hair a perfect reflection of my new excitement about what each day might hold, and strode over to my desk ready to fly through every task on the work agenda.

Before I could sit down and settle in, there was one thing I had to know: what did the coffee taste like this morning?

I'll admit it. I was beaming as I sipped at an invigorating mug full of quality coffee as I returned to my desk. Just as happy as if Josh had hand-delivered it to me himself.

I wasn't even thinking of Post-it notes and possible surprises, but there it was, floating right on top of the contents of my bag I'd left open but didn't get around to digging through earlier: a new note. A pink one.

YOU DON'T
HAVE TO CHANGE
A THING.
YOU'RE PERFECT

JUST THE WAY
YOU ARE.

Even now, it's hard to describe how those handwritten words affected me. They were *just words*, but they meant so much. They implied so much. They made me feel like I was the only woman on the planet, like all the focus was on me, like I was the center of the universe. I felt *content*, as if there was no need to worry or fuss or try so hard anymore. As if I was finally understood, appreciated.

It was incredible. Just words—but incredible.

With the pale-colored note still stuck to my fingertips, I realized I was *falling*. Falling hard for the writer—the *heart* —behind the notes.

Those silent little messages dug in deep, just drilled right through all my complaints and anxieties, my hang-ups and heartache, and warmed me from the inside out. I melted into my desk chair, slumped over my keyboard, and just stared at and into those hand-drawn characters.

I nearly sprung right *out* of my chair again when I heard Josh speak behind me.

"Having a good morning?" he asked, his morning-voice all chipper and husky. I wanted to crawl right into bed with it.

I instantly hid the note on my lap under the desk as if it was mine alone. Maybe I wanted to guard the thrill of leaving things unspoken, unaddressed in the real world. Maybe I wasn't ready to face the consequences, not yet willing to consider what the intimate messages might lead to.

I just nodded, my lips twisting up as if trying to contain a secret.

"Good..." Josh squinted at me suspiciously, his masculine face all the sexier. "What's... under your desk?"

I didn't want to talk about the notes! I wasn't ready to bring them all out in the open and... find out what was next.

"Nothing," I said, with my sexiest, most meaning-packed smile appearing on my face without my permission.

Josh gave me his own: a smile emphasizing the perfect poutiness of his full lips, his cheeks indented with dimples, and the hint of how much fun he could be if I ever got to know him all the better.

There went my body temperature again, rising to test my double dose of antiperspirant. Josh winked at me, then walked away. I almost fell out of my chair.

My heart pounded in my chest. My blouse felt tight. The fashionable silk scarf around my neck was strangling me. The small slip of paper in my hands was trembling.

I didn't know if I could handle having all the excitement I'd been longing for. But I definitely wanted to find out.

That afternoon, I was actually enjoying work. I think that's the right word for it anyway. It was fun, I plowed through the to-do list so fast, and I just felt fantastic.

Actually, I felt *perfect*. Not perfect, as in flawless, but as if everything I was, everything in my life, was just as it was meant to be. I felt worry-free, calm, happy.

I didn't know if I was changing into the person those little Post-it notes were written for or if I was just finally learning to be more comfortable as myself.

I was in love, all over again: with the hand-scrawled sentiments themselves, with how life presents little surprises, and with the person behind them all.

When I caught a glimpse of Josh over the cubicles, he didn't hesitate to smile in a way that seemed reserved just for me. It wasn't a professional smile or a polite smile. It held thoughts I couldn't wait to discover.

And I loved being the reason for an attractive man to smile like that. One of the best feelings on Earth.

Maybe that's what propelled my steps toward the break room near the end of the workday, made me take the initiative, for the first time, when I saw Josh walk in. I didn't think about it; I didn't hesitate. I just stopped in the middle of my work, took one step after the other, and found myself alone with him in the small room.

I didn't say anything; neither of us needed to. It was as if everything had been said already, in every glance, every smile, and every one of his notes.

He looked up at me when he heard me walk in. I could tell that I surprised him; I could tell it was a welcome surprise as the most amazing smile *yet* appeared on his face.

"Come for coffee?" he asked.

I smiled, even as my own confidence just started to fade.

"Let me get it for you. I've seen how hard you've been working today."

"Have you?" I asked, wondering if my answer was as forward as it sounded in my head.

Josh's gaze squinted slightly as he tried to decipher the words I didn't say. I caught myself staring at his mouth as he looked away to pour my coffee. My eyes followed the line of his strong jaw, noticed the tiny golden hairs on the nape of his neck, traveled down to his broad shoulders. I glanced away.

"Your coffee," he said, holding the mug out to me with both hands.

I reached for it quickly, just couldn't raise my eyes to

meet his again. He didn't let go of the coffee mug, even as our fingers touched.

The moment seemed to last forever. For hours, then years. So very much just in a touch.

I wanted to thank him: for every note, for every word, for how I felt. I wanted to show him how grateful I was, prove I was the woman he saw in me. But I couldn't move.

I felt his fingers detach from the mug, transferring its weight to me. I could barely hold it.

"My pleasure," he said.

I forced myself to look up, to look into his eyes, his smiling eyes. He drew in a slow breath, glanced at my own smile, and then turned to walk away.

"Josh..." I couldn't believe I spoke, couldn't believe I said his name out loud even though it ran across my own mind, unspoken, countless times before. I had no idea why I did speak, what I should say next, or what exactly I felt in that moment.

"I'm married," I said, the words sounding harsh, uninvited, but they were honest.

The smile on Josh's face didn't change. His eyes looked at me the very same way. "Okay," he said before he slipped through the doorway and stepped around the corner and out of view.

The hot coffee started to burn my hands through the sides of the mug. I set it on the counter quickly and grabbed the handle.

I didn't know why I said what I did or why then. I didn't know anything except that I was true to myself, and I felt okay. For a moment.

The commute home was another story. I was scared, but I wasn't sure what of. I was proud, confident, but uncertain that anything I did or said or thought over the last weeks was the right thing. I wondered if "the right thing" even really existed. Who's the judge of that, after all? I must be the only one truly capable of determining what's *right*, just for me, but I was also completely sure that I had no idea what that was.

I'd thought myself into a whirlwind of emotions, a royal mess of nerve endings, a tornado about to happen. I knew it as I stepped foot inside my home where Stephen innocently sat tapping at his laptop's keyboard. I knew it as I started taking it all out on him and had no desire to stop myself.

I had to vent. I had to let it all out. I had to let the pressure release, but I couldn't even admit to my own husband just why. I yelled at the air around Stephen, picking on him for anything I could think of in the moment, and I hated myself all the more for doing it—which just made me *need* to blow off more steam.

And he just took it. My husband sat there at the kitchen table, the victim of my own inner turmoil, opening his mouth as if to say something but never speaking. I can't even remember all that I shot at him in the flurry of poison-tipped, verbal barbs. But I did notice how pained he looked, how every jab at him made him wince. And I remember how small I felt: the complete opposite of all of the empowering feelings and motivations I benefited from in all the recent days. I guess I couldn't even handle my own personal growth.

I must've finally run out of things to say, ways to explain what I was feeling without divulging anything at all. When Stephen eventually spoke, his tone was so soft and careful, like a frightened child's but with more authority and conviction.

"Emily... I... I love you," he said.

And I burst into tears. I cried because he's so much more grown up than I am. I cried from embarrassment and shame; I cried for being married to a man that wouldn't even stand up to his abuser. I cried because I was that abuser: just a scared little girl left confused and frail because all the thoughts and experiences of being a woman can be just too much to bear, at any age.

And I'd passed up my one chance to share my grief—my real grief—with the one person who was supposedly my best friend and whom I knew would do everything in his power to help me find the answers.

Stephen would have devoted all the time in the world to me, but I avoided him all afternoon and evening. I chose to focus on all his weaknesses, every fault I ever perceived in him: his imperfection, his inability to read my mind, his lack of appreciation for all I suffered, for all that my marriage and husband precluded me from experiencing. I just hid away, knowing I'd have to face a new day—a workday—and, from that, there was no way to run away.

Chapter 7

A fresh start, just the hazy light of a new morning revealing itself to awakening eyes, has an almost miraculous calming effect. I woke up lying next to Stephen, who slept as soundly as ever, and I felt as if I really had purged all those poisonous, debilitating thoughts and worries. I felt empty, like I'd poured everything out and little was left, like I was ready to face the new day and carefully rebuild myself, back to some state of being that I would be happy enough with.

A good cry works wonders. I only regretted not having the comforting strength of Stephen's shoulder to do my crying on. How could I ever rebuild his impression of me after another ridiculous attack of my own self-pity?

I didn't have time to worry about it; I was already late for work. Stephen had the luxury of a flexible schedule—another something I envied him for—and dreamed his way through my hurried scampering around the bedroom. I thought about leaving him with a quick kiss on his cheek, but I was too afraid of waking him and being forced to face the repercussions of last night's one-sided argument. I ran out the door and hopped into the car, somehow managing not to forget anything.

By the time I reached the office, I felt even more calm, even meditative. I sat down at my desk, drew in a deep breath, and felt ready to accept whatever the day may hold. After all, I *was* the same woman who carried all that confidence and acted so assertively the previous days.

I glanced at that small square of yellow paper still attached to the cubicle wall above my computer monitor. I smiled at it, smiling at myself.

I finally realized all my confusion and need to lash out boiled down to one little issue: the feeling of loss. As if I *lost*, as if I lacked something. Or someone.

Someone I never had to begin with, someone I dared to imagine might be *nice* to have. Or someone I did have all along but whom I spent so much time wishing was someone else that I'd been mourning the loss of *that* fantasy for *years*.

I couldn't lose someone or something I didn't have. But even that surprisingly wise bit of self-awareness didn't prepare me for what happened next.

I was so caught up in lamenting what I thought I lost— even still letting it stew in my mind as I returned from the break room with a hot cup of coffee in my hands—that I never considered I might find a new note: another, even more intimate message that would have the capacity to open up the world of possibility all over again.

The lavender slip of paper rested in my handbag, folded in half and wedged between my makeup pouch and hairbrush. I even considered not opening it, not letting myself read the words. I had no reason to think so, but I dared to wonder if *this* Post-it would be the bearer of bad news rather than good.

It wasn't.

I DON'T MIND.
I'M CRAZY
ABOUT YOU.

I studied those little words until I'd utterly convinced myself I knew exactly what they meant, until there was only one thing they *could* mean. And when I peered up from the message resting in my hands to gaze over the expanse of cubicles all around me and saw Josh standing there, his focus on me undistracted by the swarm of coworkers buzzing around him, that meaning was confirmed.

As if my heart wasn't beating fast enough already. For the first time, I wished I committed to doing more cardio. I could die that way: pulverized by my own heightened heart rate, destroyed by the handwritten invitation to indulge in pure passion.

I smiled under the intense gaze of those blue eyes, and they didn't hesitate to smile back. That moment felt like the start of something, an agreement sealed with shared smiles.

Without losing our connection, I quickly raised my arm, flashing the Post-it at him before hiding it again on my desk, out of sight of any prying eyes. Josh raised his eyebrows and smiled more deeply before the man on his left demanded his immediate attention. My admirer looked away reluctantly, pretending his heart was in marketing rather than *me*.

I watched him at his work for a few minutes while his attention was stolen by our coworker, admiring everything about him, from his practiced posture to the way he knotted his tie. His hair was a bit more disheveled than normal, making him all the more the handsome rogue adorned in pinstripes. His dimples glinted for a moment as he chuckled at the man's joke, making me just a bit jealous that they weren't reserved just for me. But they shouldn't be. No one should be deprived of the sight of that amazing smile.

I wondered if he thought of me even then, while tied up in professional conversation. I wondered if he'd ever *say* the words he wrote for me, how I'd feel if he did. I wondered if he was actually more shy than his daring messages and flirtatious comments revealed. Or if he was the world's most skilled suitor, secretly savoring every clever step in his grand plan to seduce the object of his affection: the one woman that caught his attention.

I smiled again—at no one, at everything. And I waited to discover what was next in store for me. For *us*.

The workday forced me to wait way too long. The morning hours passed by so slowly, barely granting me one peek at Josh as he strode past the end of the hallway leading to the marketing department. I tried to distract myself with all the work I was supposed to do, but I just kept rereading those handwritten words preserved on plain paper, each one so perfectly profound.

It was agony. No, ecstasy.

I wasn't even sure just what I was waiting *for*. I had butterflies fluttering in my stomach beyond belief. Wasn't that what I wished for?

I didn't even get the chance to answer my own string of anxiety-ridden questions. Just as I counted down the minutes to when I could get away with slipping out of the office and ending the day's torture of being so near to Josh but never granted more than a passing note or a quick, flirtatious conversation, I spotted him.

Josh walked down the corridor from the marketing department and toward the supply cabinet: the perfect, private opportunity to end the anguish of secret words never spoken and suggestive thoughts revealed only in writing.

I didn't have a plan. Passion couldn't be planned. I just wanted to look into those eyes of his—those stunning, sparkling blue eyes—and see those same thoughts and intimacies revealed there. I wanted to *feel* them. Face to face.

Unlike the break room, there were no windows in the supply cabinet. No one in the entire building would be aware that the two of us met there unless a coworker walked right in. Even then, it wouldn't look remotely suspicious if we were found there. We could finally exchange words, honest words, without all the innuendo, hints, and waiting.

I don't know why I walked so quietly in that direction. I had nothing to hide and no expectations. I glided over the dingy carpet and down the corridor feeling so sure of myself, so sure of everything I felt, so in love with life in that moment.

I loved the surprises; I lived for them now. I loved how they made me feel. I loved discovering that there are men in the world that can open up like that, share their thoughts, be so sweet and tender. I loved learning that romance isn't dead. Not for me. And it never had to be again.

As I reached the end of the corridor, just a few feet from the closed door of the supply cabinet, I slowed. I realized Josh could've left already, just grabbed a box of pens or staples and returned to his desk.

I stepped forward, slipped my hand around the door handle, and pulled the door open.

My smile was instant, full of excitement and anticipation. I started to speak his name, the very sound of it so musical in my mind. Josh turned to face me, and time seemed to slow. My eyes absorbed every detail of his intense, exhilarating presence: the wisps of sandy-colored hair over his ears, framing his eyes, the sharp suit and tall stance, the curve of his lips.

His strong arms reaching around another woman's waist.

"I..." fell out of my mouth as I stared. I couldn't seem to have the ability to peel my eyes off of him. And *her*.

She was beautiful, blonde, smiling even as I stood there awkwardly staring at *her* as if she was the one that didn't belong there. I was the one that didn't belong there.

"Emily?" Josh said innocently.

I hated the sound of my name, of hearing it spoken in that situation, of being identified for my mistake in front of some other woman.

"I..." I had to do *something*. "I... I'm sorry," I said, and I finally managed to release my grip on the door handle.

Resting against the closed door, alone in the corridor, I couldn't catch my breath. It wasn't panic that stole my ability to breathe. It was disappointment. And it was deeper than any I'd ever felt in all my days or months spent lamenting the life—and love—I didn't have.

Close to tears, I pulled myself away, compelled myself back toward my desk, and I immediately gathered up all my things. Even the little yellow note pinned above my computer. I stuffed it into my purse with the others and pulled it closed, locking away all my hopes and dreams and silly wishes. I never, ever wanted to open up myself to them again.

I walked out of the building and headed straight for the car. Somehow, I made it all the way home in one piece. The time just disappeared, buried somewhere deep in my subconscious along with every consideration of Josh.

My cheeks were dry. I never shed a tear—until I saw Stephen.

When I stepped through the front door in a silent daze, my husband was just inside setting his briefcase on the table.

"My beautiful wife!" he said, his eyes shining brightly.

I fell into his arms, letting my handbag fall to the floor, and everything I never said to him and wished I could poured out in the form of tears.

"Emily... Emily..." he said softly, whispering into my ear through my mop of hair as he smoothed its length down my back.

My tears transformed into heaving sobs, and Stephen led me gently to the nearest couch to sit me down and hold me closer. He didn't ask what was wrong; he didn't pressure me to confess my shame. He didn't ask anything of me. He just gave me his full attention, all the strength that I could need.

Being in his arms felt like being home. I felt safe and even loved. Just not the kind of love that I longed for, but maybe that was just for fairytales and films and perfect women with perfect lives... and why did all those stories have to exist in the first place, teasing and taunting me for everything I felt I deserved but would never have?

It was so horribly obvious then. You just can't have the passion, the romance, and the best friend too. I certainly couldn't.

"Emily..." Stephen tried again, so calm but concerned. "What do you need? How can I make you feel better?"

I didn't have an answer. I didn't know how to make the pain go away.

"You know I love you, don't you?" he said. "What can I do for you?"

I clung to his chest, committed to soaking through his suit with my tears.

"You have to let me in," he said. "I want to make you feel better. It's my job."

I cried even harder, wondering how I could have any tears left. I knew my own silence was difficult for him; I just couldn't even formulate any words.

"Do you want to write it on a note?" Stephen asked.

I lifted my head from his shoulder.

"A Post-it?" he asked.

I stared at him, studied my husband's face and cursed the cruelty of the world for all its coincidences.

Stephen's face was expressionless; he only waited for a response. "If it's easier?"

He smiled at me, then pulled me in again for a tight hug. "You didn't even say anything about all my little notes," he whispered, unable to conceal his sadness even as he tried so hard to sound cheery. "But that's okay. I just hoped they made you happy."

My lip started to quiver, my eyes welled up with the potential for a torrent of tears. "You..." I managed to speak in the most pitiful voice.

"You found them, didn't you? In your purse? I just... I just wanted you to know what I was thinking... what you mean to me."

I pulled myself up again, still wrapped in Stephen's arms. I blinked through my tears to look at my husband more clearly, to see what I didn't see before.

"I'm crazy about you," he said with a full smile. "I can't help it. You just... make every day exciting. No matter what's going on or what we might argue about. Now..." His eyes ran over my wet cheeks, and he brushed my hair behind my shoulder. "You have to tell me what's wrong. So I can fix it for you."

The tears poured out, and I hid my face against my husband's neck as fast as possible. I squeezed him so hard and tried to catch my breath, just long enough to say, in all honesty, "Nothing. Nothing at all. Everything's just... perfect."

ALSO BY JUSTINE AVERY

NOVELS

The One Apart

NOVELETTES

The End

SHORT STORIES

Out There

Point Blank

The Darkness

Earth Inherited

It Gets Easier

Almighty

FOR ALL AGES

I Dreamed You

This Book Is Alive!

Think Outside the Box

What Wonders Await Outdoors

What Wonders Do You See... When You Dream?

This Book Wants to Make You Laugh

Everybody Poops!

Visit www.JustineAvery.com for the complete list of currently available titles, translations, and those coming soon.

ABOUT THE AUTHOR

JUSTINE AVERY is an award-winning author of stories large and small *for all*. Born in the American Midwest and raised all over the world, she is inherently an explorer, duly fascinated by everything around her and excitedly noting the stories that abound all around. As an avid reader of all genres, she weaves her own stories among them all. She has a predilection for writing speculative fiction and story twists and surprises she can't even predict herself.

Avery has either lived in or explored all 50 states of the union, over 36 countries, and all but one continent; she lost count after moving 30-some times before the age of 20. She's *intentionally* jumped out of airplanes and off the highest bungee jump in New Zealand, scuba dived *unintentionally* with sharks, designed websites, intranets, and technical manuals, bartered with indigenous Panamanians, welded automobile frames, observed at the Bujinkan Hombu Dojo in Noba, Japan, and masterminded prosperous internet businesses—to name a few adventures. She earned a Bachelor of Arts degree that life has never required, and at age 28, she sold everything she owned and quit corporate life—and her final "job"—to freelance and travel the world as she always dreamed of. And she's never looked back.

Aside from her native English, Avery speaks a bit of Japanese and a bit more Spanish, her accent is an ever-evolving mixture of Midwestern American with notes of the Deep South and indiscriminate British vocabulary and rhythm, and she says "eh"—like the Kiwis, not the Canadians. She currently lives between Los Angeles and London with her husband, British film director Devon Avery, and their adored children. She writes from wherever her curiosity takes her.

Avery loves to connect with fellow readers and creatives, explorers and imaginers, and cordially invites you to say "hello"—or *konnichiwa*.

www.JustineAvery.com
twitter.com/Justine_Avery
goodreads.com/JustineAvery
bookbub.com/authors/Justine-Avery